Growing Up Jewish With Sarah Leah Jacobs

Aaron's Bar Mitzvah

by Sylvia Rouss
Illustrated by Liz Goulet Dubois

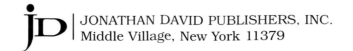

JONATHAN DAVID PUBLISHERS, INC.
Middle Village, New York 11379

To my family and friends,
for their support and encouragement
S.R.

• • •

For Mom and Dad
L.G.D.

AARON'S BAR MITZVAH

Text copyright © 2003 by Sylvia Rouss
Illustrations copyright © 2003 by Jonathan David Publishers, Inc.

No part of this book may be reproduced in any form without the
prior written consent of the publisher. Address all inquiries to:

Jonathan David Publishers, Inc.
68-22 Eliot Avenue
Middle Village, New York 11379

www.jdbooks.com

2 4 6 8 10 9 7 5 3 1

Library of Congress Cataloging in Publication Data

Rouss, Sylvia
    Aaron's bar mitzvah / by Sylvia Rouss, illustrated by Liz Goulet DuBois
      p. cm.
Summary: Sarah is unhappy because her older brother Aaron is too busy studying for
his bar mitzvah to be able to spend time with her.

ISBN 0-8246-0447-4

    [1. Brothers and sisters—Fiction. 2. Bar mitzvah—Fiction. 3. Jews—United
States—Fiction. 4. Judaism—Customs and practices—Fiction.] I. Dubois, Liz Goulet,
ill. II. Title.

PZ7.R7622Aar2003
[E]—dc21
                                          CIP
                                       2003043764

Text design and composition by John Reinhardt Book Design

Printed in China

In a few days my big brother, Aaron, will celebrate his thirteenth birthday and become a Bar Mitzvah. That means he will be old enough to read from the Torah and help lead the services at our synagogue.

Aaron's been preparing for this occasion for a long time. Today I thought he might want to read a story with me instead.

"I wish I could, Sarah, but I'm busy practicing my Bar Mitzvah prayers. Maybe you could look at a picture book with Danny."

I didn't really want to look at a book with my baby brother, but Danny was better than nobody.

I climbed over the side of Danny's playpen and showed him my book of Bible stories. When he started drooling all over Noah and the Ark, I said, "I know there's a flood in this story, but you're making the picture all soggy!"

I'd had it! I got out of the playpen just as Mommy walked into the room.

"Sarah," she said, "would you help me make chocolate chip cookies while Danny naps?"

What a silly question! That's like asking me if I want a present for my birthday! I ran to the kitchen to get ready.

Mommy mixed the dough. Then I added the chocolate chips and popped one in my mouth. "Let's make some really big cookies for Aaron!" Mommy said. I didn't want to. After all, Aaron wouldn't read with me.

I made Aaron three medium-sized cookies.

...too busy AGAIN!

The next day I asked Aaron to play ball with me. "Sarah, I'm practicing the Hebrew for my Torah portion. Why don't you go play ball with Mazel?" I didn't want to play with our neighbor's dog. He drools almost as much as Danny. But I decided that playing with Mazel was better than playing alone.

I went outdoors and threw the ball to Mazel. "Bring the ball back!" I shouted. Mazel picked up the ball and ran.

"Oh, no!" I cried. But then I remembered: It was Aaron's tennis ball. "Run, Mazel, run!" Just then Daddy came outside with a tray of red flowers.

"Would you like to help plant these, Sarah?"

"Sure," I said.

"Let's plant these in the flower box outside Aaron's bedroom window," Daddy suggested. *Good*, I thought, *maybe they'll grow into weeds*. But then I remembered that Daddy has a green thumb. The first time I heard that, I thought Daddy should wash it off, but now I know it means he is able to make things grow.

Two days later, I forgot that I was mad at Aaron. "Do you want to play a board game?" I asked him.

"Sarah, I'm practicing my *haftarah*, the story from the Prophets that I will read after the Torah portion on Shabbat. Mrs. Weiss likes board games. Why don't you ask her?"

I wondered if Aaron's *haftarah* would be about King Solomon. We learned in Hebrew school that Solomon was very smart, and even though he was busy building the Temple in Jerusalem, he still had time to answer the Queen of Sheba's riddles. I was sure that King Solomon would have played a board game with the Queen if she had asked.

Mommy said it was okay to visit Mrs. Weiss, so I walked next door and rang her bell. But she wasn't home. Aaron's tennis ball was sitting on the front porch. I picked it up and threw it into the bushes.

Suddenly, Zaydie pulled into our driveway. He stepped out of the car carrying a birdhouse. "Hi, Sarah," he called. "I made this for your mom. Where should I hang it?"

"I know the perfect spot," I said, pointing to the tree outside Aaron's window. *If a woodpecker comes along,* I thought, *that will really help Aaron practice his haftarah!*

On Friday, Bubbie and Aunt Judy came to help us prepare for Shabbat. When Aaron and I got home from school, I asked him to take a walk with me.

"Sorry, Sarah, I have to finish my Bar Mitzvah speech. Maybe Bubbie will go with you."

Bubbie was making matzah balls. "Sarah, would you like to help?" she asked. "You know how much Aaron likes matzah balls!" I hoped the matzah balls would be hard and heavy like the ones Mrs. Weiss makes.

That evening, as we ate Shabbat dinner, Aaron exclaimed, "Bubbie, these matzah balls are softer and fluffier than ever!"
"That's because Sarah helped make them," Bubbie replied with a smile.

The next day we got ready for Aaron's Bar Mitzvah. When I put on my new blue dress, I felt like a princess. "Sarah, you look beautiful!" Daddy said. I giggled and twirled around.

Bubbie, Zaydie, and Aunt Judy met us at the synagogue. Uncle Max, Bubbie's brother, gave me a big handshake. Aunt Hannah told me she had a surprise for me. I bet it's sprinkle cookies! My favorite!

During services, everyone joined in as Aaron sang the prayers. They smiled when he read his Torah and *haftarah* portions. At the end everyone said, "*Mazel tov!*"

Next, Aaron gave his speech. He thanked Mommy and Daddy, and then I heard him say, "Thank you, Sarah, for being so special."

I wondered who "Special Sarah" was. Maybe she was one of his Hebrew teachers. I looked around and saw everyone smiling at me. Did they think I was "Special Sarah?"

When Aaron thanked Sarah for making him delicious chocolate chip cookies and fluffy matzah balls, for putting up a birdhouse and planting flowers to make him feel cheerful, I knew he was talking about me, Sarah Leah Jacobs. He said I did all these things even though he hadn't had a lot of time to play with me lately. Aaron was the best big brother anyone could have!